WHAT'S GOING ON?

BY ME!

as told to Roger Hargreaves

© Mrs Roger Hargreaves 1985
Printed and published 1991 under licence from Price Stern Sloan Inc.,
Los Angeles. All rights reserved.
Published in Great Britain by World International Publishing Limited,
An Egmont Company, Egmont House, P.O.Box 111, Great Ducie Street,
Manchester M60 3BL. Printed in Germany. ISBN 0 7498 0099 2
REPRINTED 1992

A CIP catalogue record for this book is available from the British Library

Hello!

I'm Mr Nosey.

And the reason I'm called Mr Nosey
is because I am.

Mr Nosey just can't help poking
his nose into things. When he heard
that Mr Small, Mr Busy and Mr Happy
had a secret, he tried to find out what
it was - and got a surprise!

Nosey that is!

Can't help it!

Tried not to be! But I am.

Always have been. Always will be!

If ever I see a keyhole in a door, an irresistible urge comes over me and I have to peek through it.

I always want to know what's going on.

Take last week for instance.

There I was, walking along, not minding my own business, when I saw Mr Happy, Mr Small and Mr Busy.

They were standing there, talking about something.

And I wanted to know what that something was.

So, ever so quietly, I tiptoed up behind them.

I had just heard Mr Happy say,

"...and it's the day after tomorrow!"
when they saw me.

"Shh!" said Mr Small to the others.

"Hello," said I. "What were you
talking about?"

They all looked at each other in
a funny sort of way.

"It's a secret," said Mr Happy, and winked.

"Definitely," said Mr Small, and he winked

"Absolutely," said Mr Busy, and he winked too!

"Ooo," I said, hopping from foot to foot. "I love secrets!"

"But if we told you, it wouldn't be a secret, would it?" said Mr Small.

My face fell.

"Oh, all right," I said.

And went off.

But not very far.

I hid behind a tree and watched them.

There they were, talking and laughing with each other.

What was it all about?

A day-after-tomorrow secret?

What could it be?

I had to find out.

The three of them went off together, still laughing and giggling.

What was going on?

As they walked up the street they

kept looking round to see if anyone
was following them.

And I had to keep dodging into
shop doorways to make sure they
didn't see me.

And then they went into a shop.

I crept up to the shop. And I bent down under the window.

I was just about to peek into the window, when:

BUMP!

I fell flat on my face!

Well.

Actually.

I fell flat on my nose.

Which hurt!

"Ouch!" I said.

It was Mr Bump.

He'd tripped over me.

"Sorry," he said, cheerfully. "Happens all the time!"

"What are you doing anyway?" Mr Bump asked.

"I was trying to see what Mr Happy and Mr Small and Mr Busy were buying in the shop," I replied.

"Oh," said Mr Bump. "That's for the surprise!"

"What surprise?" I said eagerly.

"Aha," he winked. "It's a secret."

And off he went.

What was going on?

A day-after-tomorrow secret surprise?

I decided to go home to try and work it out.

I passed a worm.

"I don't suppose you have any idea what's going on?" I asked.

The worm winked a knowing wink.

That night I didn't sleep.

I lay awake looking at the moon.

I couldn't stand it!

Then, I had an idea!

A really good idea!

The following morning I telephoned
Mr Happy at home.

"Hello," I said in a squeaky little voice. "This is Mr Small speaking."

"No it isn't," laughed Mr Happy. "It's Mr Nosey pretending to be Mr Small speaking. What do you want?"

"Tell me what's happening tomorrow," I said. "Please," I added.

"Can't," replied Mr Happy. "It's a secret!"

"Top secret!" he added.

Oh, dear!

My really good idea wasn't.

What was going on?

What was I to do?

I waited until dark, and then I crept over to Mr Happy's house.

I could see them through the window. Mr Happy and Mr Small and Mr Busy, and Mr Bump, too.

Laughing and giggling.

I crept closer.

And closer.

And closer still!

And climbed on to
a dustbin so that I
could look in through
the window.

I couldn't quite see,
so I pulled myself up
to the window ledge.

CLANG!

I fell into the dustbin!

Ouch!

Mr Happy opened the window.

"Oh," he said. "It's you."

And he shut the window.

And drew the curtains.

And I went home.

All night long I lay in bed and wondered and wondered what the secret surprise could be.

I didn't fall asleep until just before dawn!

I was having a terrible dream about living in a country with no keyholes to look through, when I was awakened by a knocking noise.

KNOCK! KNOCK! KNOCK!

I sat up in bed.

There it was again.

KNOCK! KNOCK! KNOCK!

It was someone at the door.

I looked at my bedside clock.

It was lunchtime!

I jumped out of bed, and went downstairs.

And there they were.

Mr Happy.

Mr Small.

Mr Busy.

And Mr Bump.

"Hello, Mr Nosey," they all said.

Mr Happy was carrying a large box.

"For you," he said.

"What is it?" I asked.

"Only one way to find out," grinned
Mr Small.

What was going on?

I opened the box.

Inside was a beautiful cake.

It was shaped like a keyhole!

And it had icing on it, and a candle!

Then they all sang:

"Happy birthday to you,
Happy birthday to you,
Happy birthday Mr Nosey,
Happy birthday to you!"

So, that was it!

That was the secret surprise!

It was my birthday!

And I'd completely forgotten about it!

I'd been so busy minding other people's business, I'd forgotten my own!

Just then, Mr Muddle came up the garden path.

He looked at my birthday cake.

And then he looked at me.

"Happy Christmas," he said.